Celia's Coeliac Story

Written and Illustrated by Christiana Botziou

Cover Design by Roza Hamta

Celia Crocodile felt poorly and sad.
She didn't know why but she felt REALLY bad.
She hadn't been well and was feeling SO sick.
She felt sicky and yucky and just really ICK!

Sometimes she felt tired and so very weary.
She was anxious and worried and often got teary!
Sometimes her tummy would rumble and ache.
She could not even eat her mum's special cake!

Her throat was so sore and red ulcers were showing.
She got moody and cranky, her skin was NOT glowing.
Her lovely green scales were turning quite grey.
"That's it!" said her mum. "To the Doctor today!"

So they popped down the road to see Doctor Croc,
The very clever crocodile with rather odd socks.
"Celia will need a blood test." Doctor Croc said.
"Now off home with you and straight to your bed!"

Later that week, Celia's blood test was due.
She was so brave, she didn't get one sticker, but two!
Nurse Quack kindly told her, "You may feel a bit queasy.
Mum will look after you so just take it easy!"

A few days later, the telephone rang.
"Hello Mrs C, it's receptionist Tang.
Celia's blood test results are here.
Go see Doctor Croc and all will be clear."

So off they went to see Doctor Croc,
The very clever crocodile with rather odd socks.
"Ah do come in!" he said with a brilliant smile.
"We must get you better. You've had this for a while!"

Doctor Croc looked at Celia, "You've got Coeliac.
You've had a nasty reaction to a gluten attack."
"What's gluten?" asked Celia confused and scared.
Doctor Croc smiled kindly, his white teeth all bared.

"Gluten is a protein found in many different grains.
It helps to bind food together, but for you it's a pain!
Your body tried fighting the gluten inside,
But it needs some help from our gluten free guide.

What you need now is help from Miss Newt.
She wears big round glasses and is very astute!
She will tell you all about the right foods to eat.
So we can all help get you back on your feet."

Miss Newt told Celia about foods she could eat,
And what to avoid like barley and wheat.
There were lots of great tips and points to share
About cooking safely and being aware.

Celia's mind was blank but she felt a bit cheery.
Now she could get better and not feel so weary!
Miss Newt was very helpful about the situation,
And said that coeliac disease is a lifelong condition.

Celia and Dad then popped to the store.
There was so much choice that Celia was in awe!
They filled up their basket and paid at the till.
It was all so exciting and such a big thrill!

When Celia got home, she said "Mum can we bake?"
They made gluten free muffins and chocolate cake.
Over time Celia felt less tired and weary.
She wasn't anxious or worried and didn't get teary!

GLUTEN FREE

At school Celia told all her teachers and friends.
They were happy to hear she was now on the mend!
Now her poor tummy didn't rumble or ache.
At last she could eat some gluten free cake!

Soon it was Celia's birthday and she was turning six!
There were balloons, a bouncy castle and even magic tricks!
Everyone had such a wonderful day,
Including Celia - hip hip HURRAY!!

What is Coeliac Disease?

Coeliac disease (pronounced *see-liac*) is an illness where the body's immune system attacks its own tissues when gluten is consumed. This causes damage to the lining of the gut and means the body can't absorb nutrients properly from food. Coeliac disease is not an allergy or food intolerance.

How common is coeliac disease?

Coeliac disease affects one in 100 people. But only 30% who have the condition have been diagnosed. It can run in families but this is not always the case.

<u>What causes Coeliac Disease?</u>

Coeliac disease is caused by a reaction of the immune system to gluten, which is a protein found in wheat, barley and rye. When someone with coeliac disease eats gluten, their immune system reacts by damaging the lining of the small intestine.

<u>What are the symptoms?</u>

Symptoms of Coeliac disease can vary, but can include: diarrhoea, sickness, bad stomach pains, fatigue, irritability, and a bloated stomach.

What may happen if undiagnosed

If undiagnosed, there can be some other issues such as growth problems, anaemia and osteoporosis. If you think your child has symptoms of coeliac disease, go and see a doctor.

Treating coeliac disease

Coeliac disease is treated by maintaining a healthy, balanced gluten free diet, which will help to control the symptoms and prevent the long term consequences of the condition.

__Testing for coeliac disease__

A blood test will be carried out to check for antibodies which can indicate coeliac disease. Sometimes the blood test results can be negative yet your child may still have coeliac disease.

Your GP may refer your child to a gastroenterologist to have a gut biopsy but this is not always necessary for children.

Key Words

Biopsy-A tiny camera called an endoscope goes through your mouth and stomach into your gut.

Autoimmune disease-Your immune system attacks your body.

Coeliac disease-A digestive condition where the small intestine is unable to absorb nutrients.

Gluten-A protein found in grains like wheat, rye, and barley.

Gastroenterologist-A doctor who specialises in diagnosis and treatment of diseases of the digestive system.

Antibodies-Help us to fight off nasty, invading particles.

Immune system-Made up of special cells, to defend us against germs.

Small intestine-Absorbs most of the nutrients from what we eat and drink.

Nutrients-Found in food to help the body function.

Gut-Where your food goes after you have eaten it.

Osteoporosis-Where bones are fragile and more likely to break.

Easy Peasy Energy Bars

Ingredients

100 g walnuts finely chopped

100 g gluten free cornflakes

100 g dates finely chopped

100 g gluten free dark chocolate melted

100 g raisins

100 g dried apricots

Square or rectangular tin

Instructions

1. Put all your dry ingredients in a bowl and mix them in.
2. Melt the chocolate and pour into the bowl giving it a good mix so that all the dry ingredients are coated.
3. Line your tray with greaseproof paper. Pop the mixture evenly into your tray.
4. Put in fridge for about 15 minutes.
5. Cut the energy bars into square or rectangular shapes for you to take whenever you are on the go.

Chocolate Pig Cake
Makes an 8 inch cake round

Ingredients

4 packs Tesco Free From gluten free Belgian chocolate wafers or gluten free chocolate fingers
3 oz ground almonds
200g Gluten Free Self Raising Flour
225g butter, softened
225g (80z) Caster sugar
4 eggs
4 tablespoons natural yoghurt
3 tablespoons cocoa powder
1 teaspoon vanilla extract
For the chocolate filling and covering of cake:
200g dark or milk chocolate
1 oz Butter
2 tablespoons milk
150g icing sugar (sieved)
For the chocolate ganache
100g dark chocolate
150 ml single or double cream
1 oz butter

For the pigs I used ready to roll pink icing 250g (Sainsbury's) and edible glue

Instructions

1. Pre heat oven to 160°C/140°C Fan/Gas Mark 3. Grease and line your two 8 inch baking tins with baking paper.
2. In a large bowl, beat the butter and sugar. Add eggs and continue to beat. On a lower speed, gradually combine all the other ingredients.
3. Transfer the cake mixture evenly into the baking tins.
4. Bake for 1 hour. Check the cake is done by using the cake tester.
5. Leave to cool.
6. Over a pan of boiling water, place a bowl with the chocolate, butter and milk. Once melted, mix in the 150g sieved icing sugar to form a smooth paste.
7. Using the chocolate mixture, sandwich the cakes together, then spread the rest around the sides and a thin layer for the top.
8. Break the chocolate wafers into singular strips and place around the edge of the cake. Tie with a piece of string so that it holds the cake together until set. Put in fridge.
9. Once cool, you can make the chocolate ganache. Melt the dark chocolate and butter together and add the hot cream, making sure it is more of a liquid mixture.
10. Once it has cooled a little, pour on top of the cake to make it look like mud. Pop straight back into the fridge.
11. Take pig cake out of fridge and then you can add your piggies!
12. Tie your finished cake with a nice ribbon.

How to make the Piggies

For bathing pig

Take 20g pink icing and roll into a ball for the pigs head. Take 30g for its tummy and roll into another flatter ball. Make 4 pea sized balls for the trotters. Make a small oval shape for the snout and 2 small triangle pieces for the ears. Using a tooth pick or decorating utensils, make the indentations. Attach the ears, head and snout with edible glue.

For sitting pig

Same as bathing pig except you need 5g each for pigs arms rolled into a sausage shape. Make features for the pig using a toothpick. If pig doesn't stay upright use a toothpick to anchor it.

For pig bottoms

20g icing rolled into ball. Make an indentation using a toothpick for the bottom cheeks, and then make a little hole. Roll the fondant out into a very thin worm shape and twirl into a little tail. Attach with edible glue. You can use sugar balls for the eyes.

Pineapple upside down cake

Ingredients

For the topping
50 g softened butter
50 g light brown sugar
7/8 pineapple rings in juice, drained
handful glace cherries
1/2 tsp cinnamon
For the cake
100 g softened butter
100 g golden caster sugar
100 g gluten free self raising flour
1/2 tsp xantham gum
1 tsp baking powder
1 tsp vanilla extract
2 eggs

Instructions

1. Heat oven to 180°C /160°C fan/gas mark 4. For the topping, beat butter and sugar together until a creamy consistency. Spread over the base and about a quarter of the way up the sides of an 8 inch round cake tin. Arrange the pineapple rings on the top, and place cherries in the centre of the rings.
2. Place the cake ingredients in a bowl, with 2 tbsp of pineapple juice. Using an electric whisk, beat to a soft consistency. Spoon the mixture on top of the pineapple and smooth out so that it is level.
3. Bake for 35 mins and leave to stand for 5 mins, before turning out onto a plate.
4. Serve warm with a dollop of ice cream!

About the Author

Christiana Botziou was diagnosed with coeliac disease in 2012 after 2 years of being incredibly unwell. She decided to start a blog in 2015 to help others learn about coeliac disease and share her gluten free recipes and reviews. You can read her blog at **www.theglutenfreegreek.com.**

This is her first book.

Many Thanks To

My sister Ekaterina Botziou, for reading many drafts of this book, Roza Hamta for my wonderful cover design and my big, fat Greek family!

Goodbye!

Goodbye!

Printed in Great Britain
by Amazon